WINDOW,
MIRROR,
MOON

WINDOW, MIRROR, MOON

By Liz Rosenberg

Paintings by Ruth Richardson

Harper & Row, Publishers

Library of Congress Cataloging-in-Publication Data
  Rosenberg, Liz
  Window, mirror, moon / by Liz Rosenberg ; illustrated by Ruth
Richardson.
      p.   cm.
  "A Charlotte Zolotow book."
  Summary: A lyrical rendering of an evening—the moon, the sea, a
mirror, a baby asleep, a window, the moon—and the circle is
complete.
    ISBN 0-06-025075-5 : $ —ISBN 0-06-025076-3 (lib. bdg.) : $
  [1. Night—Fiction.] I. Richardson, Ruth, 1957–   ill.   II. Title.
PZ7.R71894Wi   1990   89-26971
[E]—dc20   CIP
                                                              AC

To Eli and David, with love eternal
—L.R.

To my mom and dad
—R.R.

In the window hung a moon,
a silver moon, a full moon.

Below the window was the sea,
a blue-black mirror, flashing.

Inside the sea swam a giant fish
with eyes as large and bright as windows.

The fish looked up through her watery world....
Above her head a crow flew by—
in his beak he held a mirror,
a tinfoil mirror he had stolen—

and then flew home.

Below his nest was a secret window.
Who's at the window? Who? Who?

Behind the window lived an owl
whose eyes were like two shining mirrors.

The owl looked out past the tops of trees,
past the path of wind,
past blowing leaves.

He stared out to a road and a car.

Between the windows sat a woman,
reading a map by a yellow light.
In her purse lay a tiny mirror

and a wallet filled with many windows:

a picture of
a house,

a picture of
a man,

a picture of
a smiling baby.

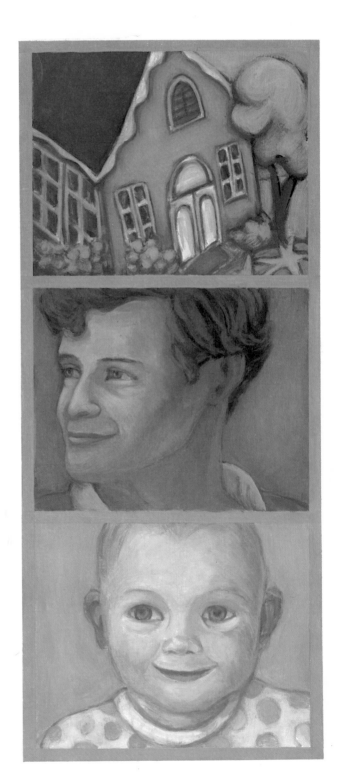

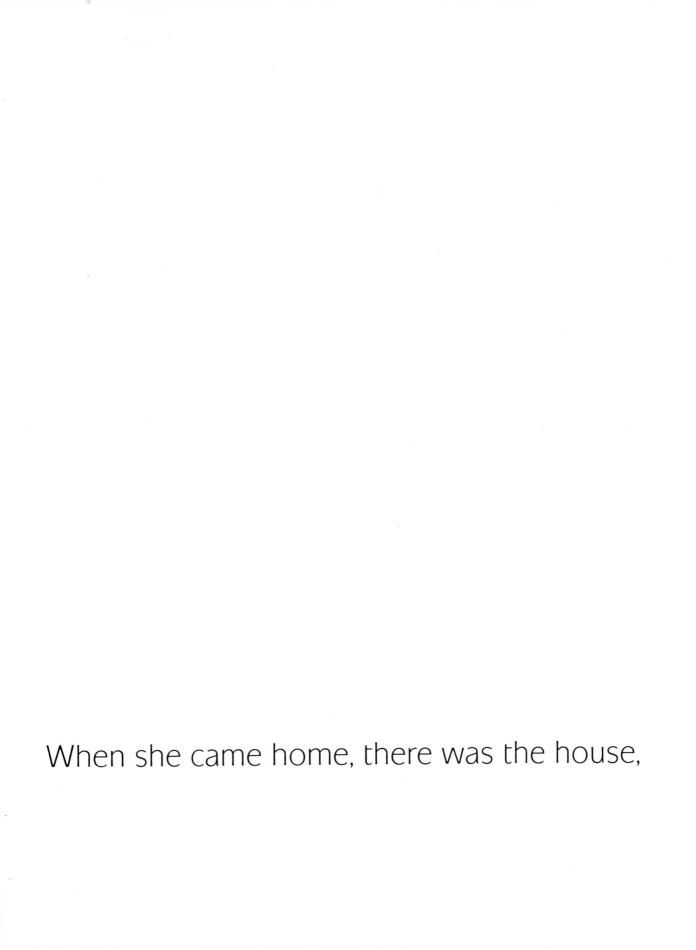

When she came home, there was the house,

and the man

and the baby!
Hush, the baby is asleep.

Above his crib hung a silver mirror.
In the mirror shone a window.

And in the window hung a moon.